Live the Adventure!

The Pit—the secret underground headquarters of the G.I. Joe Team—is your new home. That's because you are about to become a member of the world's greatest fighting force!

Your Code Name: Bombshell.

Your Major Talent: To be as explosive as your name. To battle anyone—or anything—that challenges you!

Your Assignment: To rescue a stolen mummy and the scientist who was studying it.

Two squads of G.I. Joe teams are going after the stolen mummy. Which squad will you join? Choose your teammates, Bombshell—then explode into action!

Follow the directions at the bottom of each page. Then make your decision about what to do next.

If you make the right decisions, the G.I. Joe Team will score a victory over COBRA, and you will be recognized as a hero. If you make the wrong choices—you'll wish you never left the Pit!

Good luck, Bombshell. You'll *need* it on *this* mission—which begins on page 1.

G.I. JOE

SERPENTOR AND THE MUMMY WARRIOR

BY R.L. STINE

BALLANTINE BOOKS • NEW YORK

RLI: $\dfrac{\text{VL Grades 5 \& up}}{\text{IL Grades 6 \& up}}$

Library of Congress Catalog Card Number: 87-91141

ISBN 0-345-34069-8

Interior Design by Gene Siegel

Editorial Services by Parachute Press, Inc.

Manufactured in the United States of America

First Edition: August 1987

Illustrations by David Henderson

Cover Art by Hector Garrido

FIND YOUR FATE™*

#20

G.I. JOE

SERPENTOR AND
THE MUMMY WARRIOR

"Hey, Bombshell," a voice calls to you over the clatter of dishes and loud voices in the Pit mess hall. "Grab your dish of raw meat and get a move on! You're holdin' up the line!"

You slam your tray down and turn back to the line to see who said that. Must be a rookie, you decide. Anyone who has been around the Pit for a while knows better than to give *you* a hard time!

Saying that you have a temper is like saying that Mount McKinley is a nice little hill. You didn't earn your code name, Bombshell, by being a pussycat!

You grab a plate from the shaking hand of the mess cook behind the counter and examine the gray piles of so-called food. "Uh-oh, pal," you snarl. "I warned you about those lumps in the mashed potatoes!"

"Well—" He starts to make a feeble excuse.

You don't give him a chance. You throw yourself over the counter and grab him by the throat.

You *did* warn him, after all....

Turn to page 2.

The mess cook lets out a squawk of protest as you wrestle him to the ground. *"I said no more lumps in the mashed potatoes!"* you scream.

You reach up, pull a big pan of potatoes off the counter, and push his face into it. It's the only way this turkey will learn!

"Aaaggggh!" you bellow as powerful hands pull you away from the pleading cook.

Gung-Ho and Leatherneck are trying to drag you away. "Bombshell, do you wanna end up in the stockade *again*?" Leatherneck yells.

"Get outta my face!" you scream. With a powerful burst of strength, you break free and turn to face your surprised teammates.

"Pick on someone your own size—like King Kong!" Gung-Ho says. He laughs.

You glare back at them. "Two against one," you say. "Not a fair fight. You need more help! So I'll try to go easy on you!"

With a cry of attack you lunge toward them, fists flying....

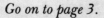

Go on to page 3.

You give Leatherneck a head butt that sends him sprawling. Gung-Ho leaps onto your back and pushes you to the kitchen floor.

"Chill out, man!" he yells. "You're too gung ho—even for me!"

"Giving up so soon, Turkey Nose?" you scream, driving a fist into his hard belly.

Still shaking his head, Leatherneck rejoins the battle. The three of you are rolling around on the floor, struggling to get the advantage.

A crowd of cheering soldiers has gathered on the other side of the counter. "Oh, man, Bombshell is at it again!" someone says.

Suddenly the cheering stops. The mess hall grows silent except for the groans and shouts of your scuffle. You look up to see that someone else has entered the kitchen.

It's that squirrelly communications specialist, Dial-Tone. "What in blazes—" he says.

"Just givin' these wimps a lesson in self-defense," you interrupt, climbing to your feet and brushing mashed potatoes off your uniform trousers.

"Lesson's over," Dial-Tone says, shaking his head. "Hawk wants to see the three of you—on the double!"

Turn to page 14.

3

"Forget the gunshots," you tell your team-mates. "That could be the way people say good morning in *this* neighborhood!" You decide to go after Zartan.

You pull the jeep through the crowd. You see the robed figure run out from the shadows, look both ways down the twisting street, then jump into a black jeep.

"He didn't see us," you say. "But I got a good look at *his* ugly mug. That's Zartan, all right. Hold on—I'm gonna run right over him!"

You floor the gas pedal. A group of farm women scream and leap out of the way of your jeep, their egg baskets flying into the air.

Turn to page 29.

The revived Huns ride into the battle with raised spears. "I don't think they know whose side they're on!" you cry. "This is *weird*!"

"Who cares?" says Mainframe, studying something on his computer. "Let's take advantage of this little dispute—and get outta here!"

A few seconds later your two Mauler tanks are roaring away, following the riverbank, unnoticed by the battling COBRAS. "According to my tracking unit," Mainframe says, his eyes on the screen, "the structure that Dr. Wilmott and the mummy are being held in is over that rise."

"With all these COBRA big shots here, it might be heavily guarded," Sci-Fi warns.

A long, low structure of unpainted light wood comes into view. "This is the HQ," Mainframe says.

"I don't see any guards," you tell him, peering out of the tank. "I don't see *anybody*! You sure this ain't somebody's garage?"

"It's no garage," Mainframe says seriously. He radios Flint in the other tank. "Hey, Flint—are we goin' in?"

There is a little static on the radio. Then you hear the steady voice of Flint: "We're goin' in...."

Turn to page 36.

Serpentor walks over to the mummy. "For so many centuries this great warrior has rested," Serpentor says. "Now at last he and I will be reunited. And with Wilmott's brilliant mind inside him, Tutanh Harmak will be more than a warrior. He and I will be *invincible*!"

"You mean that *COBRA* will be invincible —don't you, Serpentor?" Mindbender asks suspiciously.

Serpentor ignores his question. "Hurry, Mindbender," he says sharply. "After you have brought Tutanh Harmak back to life, I want you to use the brain scanner on our high-spirited G.I. Joe friend here!"

Turn to page 83.

"It's a coin toss," Flint says grimly. "But let's believe this message is for real. Mainframe, radio Hawk. Tell him that our new destination is the Swiss Alps. Tell him we need plenty of sky support."

A few seconds later Mainframe connects to the Pit. Hawk is skeptical. He thinks the whole thing may be a COBRA trick. "But let's fill the air with Skystrikers just in case," Hawk says.

"Hey, Hawk—think ya could remember to send my skis?" you yell into the radio.

Flint shoves you back into your seat. "Bombshell," he says angrily, "if you don't shape up, I'm gonna ski down the Alps on *you*!"

You look up at him. He *really* means it! You decide to take a nap the rest of the way to Switzerland!

Turn to page 49.

"Get down!" you scream as a storm of arrows batters the jeep. The four of you hit the sand and crawl behind the vehicle.

Roadblock fumbles in his pack and pulls out a grenade. "Here—catch, you turkeys!" he yells, heaving it at the whooping barbarian army. The explosion topples several soldiers. Their war whoops turn to howls of surprise.

A second grenade misses the mark. But your foes pull their horses back a few paces. You keep them back with a steady blast of rifle fire.

"Hey, what're they doin'?" Leatherneck yells. They've pulled their horses into a single line. Their long-haired leader lowers his arm and points forward.

"Oh, boy—here they come!" you yell. "They're gonna ride right over us!"

Turn to page 20.

You follow the tunnel for what seems like hours. It twists and takes you deeper down. The air gets hotter and heavier.

The tunnel opens into another low, empty cavern.

"Haven't we been here before?" Leatherneck asks.

"Keep movin'," you say. "This has gotta lead somewhere. We can't keep goin' in circles forever—*can* we?"

Turn to page 31.

Your anger gives you strength beyond your normal powers. With a scream of fury, you punch the gun from the surprised scientist's hand, grab him, and heave him at Mindbender's giant electronic machine.

As he crashes into the machine with shattering force, Wilmott cries out. The machine lets out an eerie answering squeal, and sparks fly out in all directions. The sparks grow into a vibrating purple-blue ribbon of electric current.

"*Aaaiiiii!*" Wilmott is enveloped in the current.

You stare in horror. There is nothing you can do to save him.

And then—you see the mummy begin to move!

Turn to page 42.

"No—we won't kill them," Destro insists, his voice muffled behind the silver mask he always wears. "Why waste perfectly good bodies? Mindbender can use them."

So the notorious COBRA scientist, Dr. Mindbender, is involved in this, along with Serpentor, that new COBRA warrior you've heard about. What on earth are they all up to in this damp mosquito trap?

You decide there's only one way to find out.

With a burst of strength, you pull away from the Crimson Guard who is holding you.

Now—whom will you attack?

Destro? Turn to page 22.
Zartan? Turn to page 32.

You drag Destro to his feet. Gung-Ho shoves a machine gun into his ribs. Destro sees that he has no choice. Holding his aching throat, he leads you into the pyramid.

You practically choke on the thick musty air. Crumbling yellow bricks form a labyrinth of narrow corridors. The dust on the floor is at least six inches deep.

Destro leads you through the ancient maze. He pushes a bright orange brick, and a tunnel entrance slides open. He leads you down the tunnel. You finger your weapon nervously and keep it ready. Is he leading you into a trap?

Turn to page 43.

"Too bad, Bombshell," Gung-Ho says as you head toward the secret briefing room on the third level of the Pit. "You didn't get your lunch."

"Sure I did." You sneer. "I had you two guys for lunch!"

Your two teammates look as if they're ready to start up the fight again. But you've reached the briefing room. You push open the door and are greeted by a grim-faced Hawk. "Take a seat, men," he says.

Several other G.I. Joe Team members are already seated around the long conference table. Hawk stands at the far end, scratching his blond hair as if trying to decide where to begin.

"We've got a little problem to attend to," Hawk says. "I want to show you some pictures." He pulls down the wall screen. Dial-Tone turns on the slide projector. He focuses the first slide —an Egyptian mummy.

"Hey, I want my mummy!" you yell.

A few guys laugh. Hawk glares at you, the way he always glares at you when you wisecrack during briefings. "Bombshell," he says quietly, "don't make me sorry I removed your leash!" He looks back at the mummy. "This is serious, guys. COBRA may be involved."

....

Go on to page 15.

Hawk taps his pointer against the screen. "This is the remains of an ancient Egyptian warrior," he says. "His name was Tutanh Harmak. Until last week he resided at the National Museum in Cairo. Last week Tutanh Harmak was stolen from the museum."

The next slide comes on the screen. It shows a middle-aged man with thinning blond hair and a closely trimmed blond beard and mustache. "This is Dr. Everson Wilmott," Hawk says, tapping the man's nose with the pointer. "He's an American scientist. Wilmott had been doing radiocarbon dating tests on the mummy. He was kidnapped along with the mummy.

"The materials Wilmott was using were radioactive," Hawk continues. "So army intelligence scientists were able to trace the mummy's whereabouts. It's in the desert outside Cairo. Surveillance planes have shown some sort of newly built structure there, a large building of some sort."

"Is COBRA behind this?" Gung-Ho asks.

"We don't know," Hawk says, rolling up the screen. "But we're gonna find out!"

Turn to page 24.

"I know that your hobby is busting up things, Bombshell," Flint says to you. "But we're in a bit of a hurry." He turns to Mainframe. "Do you get a reading on your tracer unit?"

Mainframe studies the small screen. "If my coordinates are correct," he tells Flint, "the mummy has been moved to one of the large pyramids in the desert outside the city."

Without any further delay, you pile into the A.W.E. Strikers and head toward the pyramid. Waves of heat make the desert shimmer. The white sand sparkles under the blinding sun. When the pyramid appears, looming taller than you had imagined, it seems unreal, like a vision or a mirage.

But the COBRA Crimson Guards that come running forward to defend the pyramid are real enough! The desert quiet is shattered by the deafening roar of weaponfire.

It's all over in a minute. The Crimson Guards have been defeated. You run across the hot sand to the pyramid entrance—

—just as a silver-masked figure comes running out. It's the COBRA weapons dealer, Destro!

He isn't expecting anyone. You take him by surprise, leaping on top of him. He topples helplessly to the sand.

"Don't flatten him, Bombshell," Flint calls. "We may need him!"

....

Turn to page 53.

You drop back quickly, bring your foot up swiftly, and kick the pistol out of Wilmott's hand.

It twirls end over end, high in the air—

—and then sails down, right into Serpentor's waiting hand. He points the gun at you and laughs gleefully.

"What the heck," you say. "I wasn't a punter. I was a defensive tackle!"

Unfortunately, Bombshell, the triumphant Serpentor is about to see that you have a *new* position—

THE END!

You follow the river according to the coordinates mapped out by Mainframe. Your vehicle glides easily over the silent shifting sands. All is tranquil. You see no sign of danger, no evidence of any nearby enemy forces.

Nearly an hour later, you arrive at a long, low structure built into a hill overlooking the brown waters of the Nile. Gung-Ho runs out of the building to greet you. "It's deserted!" he yells. "The whole building is as empty as Bombshell's head!"

"Now, wait a minute—" you growl, raising a fist.

"Easy, fella," Flint warns. "Let's go inside and have a look-see."

Turn to page 39.

The barbarians' primitive war whoops fill the air as they charge. Roadblock heaves another grenade, then another. But there are too many of them to be stopped by a few puny grenades and three meager assault rifles.

Some of the horses stumble in the dry yellow sand. But the line closes up and the charge continues.

Suddenly you hear an approaching rumble from the riverbank. You turn and see a familiar sight—two four-man Mauler M.B.T. tanks—barreling your way. "Well, well...our buddies have finally decided to join the party!" you cry.

"Watch these barbarian turkeys head for the hills!" Roadblock says, staring at the approaching tank. "Sci-Fi's done a job on the Mauler. He's got a laser cannon in place!"

A silent red beam of brilliant laser light shoots over the sand. The barbarians grow silent. Their mouths drop open in amazement. Frightened horses whinny and rear up. A second laser blast is all they need to convince them the battle is over!

Without waiting for a signal from their leader, the terrified soldiers pull their horses around and flee, galloping off in all directions.

....

Go on to page 21.

"Who *were* those cowboys?" Flint asks, poking his head from the hatch of one of the Maulers. "I thought maybe someone was making a movie!"

"It wasn't any movie," you tell him. "They were playin' for keeps."

"Good thing the cavalry arrived in the nick of time," Flint says, removing his familiar green beret and mopping his forehead with it.

"Maybe..." you say, looking past the two G.I. Joe tanks at a cloud of sand approaching across the desert. "But it looks like we've got more Indians on the way!"

You and your buddies on the assault team quickly pile into the Mauler tanks. But there is no time to escape. A squadron of more than thirty COBRA Ferrets—all-terrain missile-carriers—wheels over the sand and quickly surrounds you.

Surrender? Turn to page 58.

Blast them with the laser cannons? Turn to page 68.

You lunge toward Destro. He swings out of your way. You fly past him. Your head collides with the wall. Everything goes black.

When you regain consciousness, you are wearing a ragged brown uniform. A longbow is draped over your shoulder. A quiver of arrows is at your side.

How did this happen to you? Why are you dressed like one of the barbarian soldiers? What have they done to you?

You do not care. Your mind has been wiped clean of such questions.

You pick up your spear and walk quickly to join your fellow soldiers....

THE END

Coming at you on horseback is the strangest-looking army you've ever seen! Dressed in ragged brown robes, their hair down to their shoulders, the soldiers, screaming like banshees, hold primitive spears over their heads as they charge.

"Who is this—Attila the Hun?" you scream. "Are they for real?"

A spear whistles by, inches from your head. They're for real!

"Let's get outta here!" Leatherneck yells. "Turn the jeep around, Bombshell!"

"Nothin' doin'," you tell him. "I'm not retreating from these *barbarians*! I'll shout 'boo' and they'll run away!"

But you realize you've got to do more than shout "boo"—especially since you're outnumbered about two hundred to four!

Should you pile out of the jeep and use it for cover as you battle the onrushing barbarian army? Or should you stay in the jeep and try to drive right through them?

Jump out of the jeep and start your attack? Turn to page 44.

Try to drive through them? Turn to page 54.

"The G.I. Joe Team has been asked to find out why the mummy and the scientist were taken from the museum—and to rescue both of them," Hawk says.

"Yo, Joe!" Gung-Ho yells, ready for some action.

"We're sending two teams to Cairo," Hawk tells you. "First an assault team, then a technical backup squad."

"Which team am I on?" you ask eagerly.

"Not mine, I hope!" yells Leatherneck.

"Not mine, either!" yells the computer expert, Mainframe.

Everyone in the room knows you're a great fighting man. But they also know you'll fight with *anyone*—or *anything*!

"*You* choose," Hawk says. "I don't care *which* team you go on, Bombshell. I just want you outta the Pit—and outta my hair!"

Which team will you choose to go with?

Go on to page 25. Read the personnel list for each team. Then make your choice.

G.I. JOE CAIRO MISSION TEAMS

Assault Team	*Technical Team*
Leatherneck	Flint
Gung-Ho	Mainframe
Roadblock	Sci-Fi

The assault team is made up of three of the toughest fighters ever to wear the G.I. Joe uniform. You'd fit in well with this team.

The technical team includes a Rhodes scholar, a computer genius, and a laser-weapons expert. The team could use some muscle—namely *you*.

Which team will you travel to Egypt with?

If you choose the assault team, turn to page 40.

If you choose the technical team, turn to page 50.

You open fire with everything you've got. The COBRA Rattlers return your fire. A sky-striker explodes in a ball of flame. Two Rattlers, struck by rockets, plummet in fiery streaks to the cliffs below.

"I can't figure it," Flint says as a COBRA rocket explodes dangerously near your jet. "Such a *big* air assault squad just to protect a stolen mummy?"

You grab the rocket launcher controls. "Let's clear these clowns outta here so we can get to the bottom of this!" you yell.

The COBRA combat jets inflict damage, but the G.I. Joe Skystrikers prevail. Two more Rattlers fall to the snow. The few remaining enemy planes roar away in retreat.

"*Yo, Joe!*" goes up the triumphant cry.

A few seconds later you eject from the plane and parachute through the icy winds to the cliff that hides the COBRA fortress.

You land with assault rifles blazing and take out the astonished fortress guards. You blast away the steel entrance door and run inside. More Crimson Guards await you. The long corridor rings with weaponfire. "They're guarding more than a mummy in here!" you yell.

But what?

Turn to page 59.

Your usual plan of attack is to strike first, think later. That's the strategy you use as you lunge at Serpentor. You grab the serpent-toothed hood that circles his face and try to pull him to the floor.

He ducks out of your grasp and leaps back. "Fool!" Serpentor cries. "I am cloned from the ten greatest warriors in history! Do you really think you're a match for me?"

In reply to his question, you drive your fist deep into his solar plexus. He makes a choking sound and staggers back.

Have you defeated this great warrior so easily?

Turn to page 67.

Zartan has spotted you now—thanks to your subtle maneuver. His jeep lets out a roar as it picks up speed. His tires squeal as he makes a sharp turn into a hidden alley. But you keep right behind him.

Soon you are out in open desert. Zartan's tires kick up a blinding wall of sand.

Suddenly he squeals to a stop. Reflexively, your foot hits the brake too. Your jeep makes a complete circle as it spins to a stop. As the sand settles and the air clears, you see a terrifying sight.

"Holy macaroni!" you yell. "Looks like Zartan led us right into a trap!"

Turn to page 23.

"Yo, Joe! Let's fight these weirdos off!" Gung-Ho shouts. Good old Gung-Ho. When it comes to fighting, he can always be counted on to be as insane as *you* are!

"Yo, Gung-Ho!" you yell, raising your assault rifle.

"I can't believe I'm the rational one in this group," Roadblock says, shaking his head. "You turkeys—we're outnumbered about two million to one! We gotta find a boat—or swim for it!"

He doesn't wait to discuss it. He slides down the sandy embankment toward the river and begins prowling the leafy underbrush in search of a boat or a canoe. You lower your rifle and follow Roadblock to the water. You'd never admit it, but you know he's right.

There's only one small problem, you quickly discover. No boat. No canoe.

No escape.

You look to the top of the embankment and see that the ragged barbarian warriors have dismounted and are headed toward you.

Turn to page 45.

"Maybe we oughta head back," Mainframe suggests as a low cavern leads into another tunnel. You seem to be descending into another chasm of tunnels.

"It's endless! Endless!" Gung-Ho complains.

But it can't be endless—*can* it?

Turn to page 51.

You lunge at Zartan, connecting your powerful right fist with his jaw. He staggers backward, his eyes wide with surprise.

Gung-Ho, Leatherneck, and Roadblock struggle to free themselves. But guards shove rifles into their bellies to keep them from coming to your aid.

Zartan lowers his head and runs at you. You grab him by the shoulders and spin him around, then land a punch in his midsection. He drops to his knees.

You see Destro coming at you. You spin around to face him—and a Crimson Guard brings the butt of his rifle down on the back of your head.

As you shake the flashing stars from your head, two guards push you up against the wall. You see that someone else has been watching the fight from the shadows.

He steps forward. He is wearing a viper-toothed cowl shaped like a serpent's head. It is Serpentor!

"Very impressive," Serpentor says sarcastically.

"Shucks, that was nothin'," you tell him. "Why don't you step over here, Snake Face, and I'll show you what I can *really* do!"

Turn to page 79.

Serpentor takes a step forward as you run to attack him. To your surprise he turns you around by the shoulders, bends you back, and brings a knee up hard into the small of your back.

You cry out in shock and pain.

"Fool!" he says contemptuously. "Do you not know that I am made of the ten greatest warriors in history?"

You struggle to regain your feet, but the pain is overwhelming. You can't get up.

Serpentor runs to the brain scanner machine—and throws the switch. The machine roars into motion. *"Aaaiiii!"* Dr. Wilmott screams in agony as his brain cells are copied and transferred to the ancient mummy.

Ignoring the pain, you stand up. All eyes are on the mummy. The machine whirrs. Dr. Wilmott's head slumps forward in a faint. And the mummy begins to walk!

Slowly the ancient mummy lurches forward. "Welcome, my old friend. Welcome!" Serpentor shouts triumphantly, grinning behind his serpentlike mask. He runs up to greet his old comrade. "You may begin your glorious new career," Serpentor tells the mummy, "by killing that G.I. Joe idiot!"

Turn to page 47.

As you look on helplessly, the mummy staggers to life and moves forward on its unbending legs, its spindly arms outstretched like a sleepwalker's.

Mindbender's machine has worked. The ancient Egyptian, who alone knows the secret of the pyramid's awesome powers, lives again!

The mummy takes another silent step, then another. Serpentor, grinning like a madman, steps forward to offer it greetings of welcome. He puts out a hand.

The mummy takes Serpentor's hand and begins to twist it!

"Let go at once!" Serpentor commands.

The mummy continues to twist Serpentor's hand. Serpentor struggles to free himself. He lets out a cry of surprise as he realizes that the mummy is stronger than he is!

Serpentor howls in pain. The mummy continues his one-handed attack. With a gasp, Serpentor manages to break free.

He flees from the pursuing mummy, along with Mindbender and the COBRA Crimson Guards.

You step forward, prepared for a fight. Will the mummy attack *you* next?

Turn to page 57.

You and your G.I. Joe teammates pile out of the tanks, your assault rifles at the ready. The sun is high in the sky. You feel hot and uncomfortable. You look over at the rolling waters of the Nile. You wish you could jump in and go for a swim.

"Where's the welcome party?" you ask. You raise your rifles and make your way cautiously to the single door at the side of the long building. Roadblock kicks in the door with one swipe of his size 14 combat boot.

"Anybody home?" you call. There's no answer. You and your buddies burst into a dark corridor. Two sleeping Crimson Guards stir from their positions on the floor. You use the butt of your rifle to make sure they continue to get their rest.

Now the seven of you are jogging down the corridor, which runs the length of the building. You pass by living quarters, a laboratory filled with electronic machines, a mess hall—all deserted. "Guess they've all joined the fight between Serpentor and Mindbender," Flint says.

At the end of the corridor, you storm into a small chamber. A dim bulb suspended from the ceiling provides the only light. Beneath the bulb stands the mummy. And in its shadow, tied to a chair, is Dr. Everson Wilmott.

....

Go on to page 37.

A few seconds later a grateful Dr. Wilmott has been untied. "This has been a horrible, horrible experience," he says, his voice trembling with anger—and weariness.

"Dr. Wilmott, what did COBRA want with you?" Flint asks. "Why were you kidnapped? Why were you and the mummy brought here?"

The scientist shrugs, frowning. "I have no idea," he says. "None at all. No one said a word to me."

You've come a long way for no answers. What did COBRA intend to do in this deserted headquarters? Why did they need the scientist and the mummy?

Perhaps you'll learn the answers in other adventures. But for now you don't care. Dr. Wilmott and his ancient treasure will soon be safe and sound. Mission not explained—but mission accomplished.

You stare at the priceless mummy. "Hey, Doc," you say, "do you ever get too wrapped up in your work?" You laugh until you nearly split a gut. But what's with your unsmiling buddies? No sense of humor? Guess you're just too cryptic for them!

THE END

"Sounds like a phony to me," Flint says. "Why isn't the message in code? Somebody *wants* us to understand it. We're keeping on course to Cairo!"

You deplane on a hidden airstrip on the outskirts of the city. Sci-Fi readies his laser machine pistol. Mainframe is in contact with the assault team, which landed an hour before you. They have already reached the mysterious building on the banks of the Nile.

You climb into a waiting A.W.E. (All-Weather and Environment) Striker. It's no bigger than a jeep, but it carries a top-mounted cannon. You start up the powerful engine and roar off to catch up with your buddies on the assault team.

Turn to page 19.

You follow Gung-Ho into the deserted building. You find piles of dirty COBRA uniforms, half-eaten food, warm water in a metal bathtub—signs that COBRA was here, maybe less than two or three hours ago.

"They moved out quickly," Flint says. "We'd better move quickly after them."

"Hey, come on," you interrupt. "Let's wreck the joint first! Whaddaya say?"

"Yeah!" Gung-Ho agrees. "Yo, Bombshell! Let's make sure they can't come back here!"

"We don't have time," Mainframe argues. "Dr. Wilmott may be in danger."

Which will it be?

Wreck COBRA headquarters? Turn to page 62.
Leave quickly and go after the COBRAS? Turn to page 16.

Two hours later a G.I. Joe transport plane is in the air, carrying you and the other three members of the assault team to Cairo. "Hey— my seat is broken!" you cry. You jump to your feet, turn, and rip the seat out of the floor.

"You shouldn't'a done that, Bombshell," says Roadblock. "Now you gotta stand the rest of the way."

"No, I don't," you reply, leaning over him menacingly, "'cause I'm gonna take *your* seat, Chicken Face!"

Roadblock leaps to the challenge. His massive hands go for your throat. The two of you begin to scuffle in the narrow plane aisle.

"Knock it off, Bombshell," Gung-Ho yells. "Is fighting the only way you can kill time? Why don't you read a book instead?"

You turn and sneer at Gung-Ho. "I already read a book once," you tell him.

Everyone laughs.

Before you know it, you've landed in Cairo. You come down on a hidden airstrip on the outskirts of the city. You step out into hot sunlight. The air feels heavy and wet. You climb behind the wheel of a waiting jeep and head for Cairo —and the unknown....

Turn to page 76.

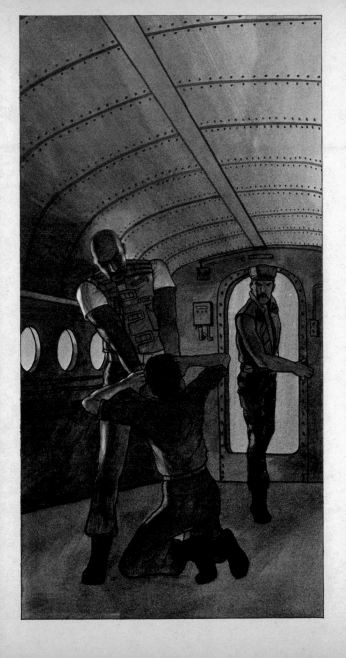

The mummy staggers forward. It seems to take one step, then another.

"*It's alive!*" you scream.

But you immediately realize your mistake. Tutanh Harmak has not come to life. The electricity surging from the machine is propelling the mummy forward.

You hear a loud crackle and see a blaze of white light as an even more powerful surge of electricity thrusts into the ancient mummy from the metal hood on its head.

The mummy takes one final staggering step and falls to powder on the pyramid floor.

You look up to see that your buddies have defeated the COBRAS, and Serpentor and Mindbender have fled. Flint runs over to you. "What happened?" he asks, pointing at the mummy.

You shrug. "Looks like he took a powder!" you say.

It's not the best joke you ever made. But you laugh long and hard at it anyway. Is anyone else laughing? You don't care. Mission is accomplished. You're heading home!

THE END

Destro stops at the end of the tunnel. A narrow opening leads into a large room. You pause before you reach it and listen silently to the voices coming from inside. As your eyes adjust to the light, you see the mummy and Dr. Wilmott in the room. And standing beside them are the notorious COBRA mind-control scientist, Dr. Mindbender—and Serpentor, the warrior Mindbender constructed from the cells of the world's ten greatest warriors!

"Mindbender," Serpentor says in a booming voice that echoes again and again off the ancient pyramid bricks, "when will the awesome, unconquerable powers of the pyramid be mine?"

"Soon, Serpentor," Mindbender replies gravely. "Soon...."

Turn to page 75.

You and your teammates leap from the jeep and raise your assault rifles. "Don't take any prisoners!" you yell.

"Hey, Bombshell—I like your attitude!" Gung-Ho says, grinning. "You're the squirrelliest guy I—"

Gung-Ho doesn't get to finish his sentence, because the four of you suddenly realize that you are surrounded on all sides by the barbarian soldiers. The battle is over before it has begun. Even with your automatic rifles, you are no match for the hundreds of primitive warriors.

With spears pointed against your chests, you reluctantly toss down your weapons. Zartan steps forward, grinning triumphantly behind the black and white makeup that always covers his face. "Welcome," he says with a sneer. "I hope you will allow me to show you boys some COBRA hospitality!"

Turn to page 84.

Suddenly a strange figure steps out in front of the approaching army. He wears a long, flowing yellow cape. His face is circled by a green serpent's-head cowl, its venomous fangs framing his forehead.

Serpentor!

Hawk held a briefing on this new COBRA menace a few months before. According to Hawk, Serpentor was created by the COBRA mind-control scientist, Dr. Mindbender. He is made from cells of the ten greatest warriors of all time.

At the time you thought the whole story was a slice of grade-A baloney. But staring up into the serpent-hooded face of this new foe, you have the feeling it could be true.

"Prepare to die, fools!" Serpentor yells down to you.

He raises his arm—a signal to his ragged army. They roar out a deafening battle cry, lift wooden longbows, and take aim.

Turn to page 64.

"*Mindbender!*" Serpentor screams, lifting the COBRA scientist off the ground by the throat. "Mindbender, those puny Huns you created to be my soldiers—they let me down!"

Dr. Mindbender raises his muscular arms and pulls Serpentor's hand off his throat. His face grows red with fury and he shakes a powerful fist in Serpentor's face. "Listen to me, Serpentor," Mindbender bellows. "Don't forget that *you* are my creation too! Do not vent your anger on me! You have sworn allegiance to COBRA—and *I* am part of COBRA!"

Serpentor sneers behind the green snake mask that hoods his face. "I have sworn allegiance to no one!" he declares. He shoves Mindbender to the ground.

"You power-hungry fool!" Mindbender yells.

Suddenly shots ring out. The COBRA Ferrets have begun firing at one another! You watch as Mindbender pulls himself up quickly and retreats to his vehicle. "Hey—they're fightin' each other!" you cry gleefully. "It's Serpentor's guys against Mindbender's guys!"

As the COBRA Ferrets circle one another, firing their weapons, you see a line of horses galloping to the scene. The Huns are coming back for more!

Turn to page 5.

46

"Now, hold on a minute, old buddy—" you yell, taking a step toward the door. A Crimson Guard moves up, his machine pistol raised, to keep you from going any farther.

The ancient mummy, its arms outstretched, creaks toward you. Then, with startling speed, it wheels around—

—and grabs Serpentor by the throat!

Serpentor wheezes out a protest and tries to squirm from the mummy's grasp. Mindbender comes at the mummy, trying to help Serpentor. But you pile into Mindbender and send him sprawling to the floor.

Serpentor struggles to grip the mummy, but the ancient warrior is too powerful for him. The mummy lifts Serpentor off the floor and heaves him against the wall.

With a cry of surprise, Serpentor touches a wall panel. A hidden door opens, and Serpentor disappears behind it. "Hey—wait for me!" Mindbender calls.

He scrambles to his feet and heads out the laboratory door into the waiting hands of Leatherneck, Roadblock, and Gung-Ho!

"Hey—what'll we do with this guy?" Gung-Ho asks.

"I don't know," you tell him, smiling. "Wait for the next garbage pickup, I guess...."

Turn to page 88.

47

Dr. Wilmott, his blue eyes flaring with hatred, pushes the pistol into your ribs. "You imbecile!" he cries. "Where do you think Mindbender got all the information about Tutanh Harmak? From *me*, of course!"

You look down at Wilmott's gun and see a familiar insignia tattooed on his hand. Dr. Wilmott is a COBRA!

Fury builds inside you as you realize you have risked your life to rescue the enemy. You've got to act. You can't let Wilmott get away with making fools of the G.I. Joe Team!

Do you try to kick the pistol out of the scientist's hand? Turn to page 18.

Do you lift the scientist off the ground and heave him at Mindbender's machine? Turn to page 10.

The Alps don't look real from the plane window. They look like an oil painting of whites and purples.

A fleet of G.I. Joe Skystriker combat jets roars out of the clouds to back you up. Mainframe charts the course, using the coordinates in the intercepted COBRA message.

"Hey, look!" Flint yells. "There's a fortress down there. It's hidden behind the tall pines on that low cliff. All planes—assume battle readiness!"

It's good advice. Suddenly the blue sky turns black. Dozens of black COBRA Rattlers, armed with combat rockets and cluster bombs, roar toward you.

"Looks like we ain't flyin' the friendly skies!" you yell.

Turn to page 27.

49

A few hours later a supersonic jet streaks through the skies, carrying you and the other three members of the technical team to Cairo. Flint sits silently in the seat in front of you, poring over maps of the region. Mainframe busily types away at his computer console. Sci-Fi reads a laser technology report, underlining sentences in yellow.

"Hey—what a fun group *I* picked!" you bellow. "How 'bout a little gin rummy, guys?"

Everyone ignores you.

"C'mon, let's liven things up!" you shout. "Anybody know a good joke—you know, the kind ya can't tell your mother! Ha ha!"

Silence.

"Well, I got one," you insist. "It seems there was this rabbit who—"

"I'm intercepting a strange message here!" Mainframe calls from the back of the plane.

"You're interruptin' my joke—that's what you're doing!" you snarl. "Do I have to teach you smart guys some manners?"

"Chill out, Bombshell," Mainframe says angrily. "Flint, I think you'd better read this. Looks like it's from COBRA!"

Turn to page 66.

You keep walking. The air is so hot and thick, it's hard to breathe.

"Look—footprints!" Leatherneck cries.

"I think those are *our* footprints," Flint says, bending low to examine them.

"Let's keep going," you say impatiently. "I know we can find a way outta here. I *know* it!"

Turn to page 9.

The Crimson Guards leap at you, but you break away and head straight to Dr. Wilmott. You rip off the metal hood and tear away the straps that hold him down. "Come on, Doc— let's move!" you yell, pulling his arm.

But Wilmott resists. "I can't," he says. "I can't leave the mummy."

"*Wh*—?" you cry in disbelief. "Are you outta your ever-lovin'—"

The Crimson Guards grab you. One gives you a karate chop to the neck that sends you crashing to the floor. They drag you off to a corner of the lab.

Dr. Wilmott is returned to the seat of honor, and the hood is pulled down over his head. You look away angrily as Mindbender prepares to pull the switch that will copy Wilmott's brain waves and transfer them to the mummy.

The crackle of electricity gives you a sick feeling in the pit of your stomach. Your brain is next, after all. Well...your buddies have always said that you're "out of your mind." It looks like you're about to prove it!

THE END

You grab Destro by the throat and begin to squeeze. "Where are Wilmott and the mummy?" you demand.

He is silent. You grasp his throat a little tighter. He sees that you mean business.

"Stop—please!" Destro gasps behind the silver mask that hides his face from the world. You loosen your grip enough to let him speak. "The mummy—I—just delivered it."

"Where?" you demand, tightening your grip once again. "Take us to it—now!"

Turn to page 13.

"I ain't gettin' outta this jeep!" Gung-Ho yells. "Keep drivin', Bombshell!"

As you floor the gas pedal, the barbarian leader yells a command, and a barrage of spears darkens the sky.

You swerve sharply to the right, and the spears fall to the sand with a deafening clatter. "*Nyyaaah*! Ya missed me!" you yell.

But there is no time to celebrate. Whooping in unison, the strange soldiers raise longbows. The next barrage will be deadly arrows.

"Drive right through! Drive right through!" Gung-Ho screams from the backseat.

"Whaddaya think I'm *tryin'* to do?" you yell back to him. "Parallel park?"

An arrow shatters the windshield. Another punctures the hood.

The jeep roars as you force it forward, the tires whining as they slide in the sand. The sand is everywhere now—on the ground, in the air. You cannot see. You can only hear. You hear the pounding of horse hooves, the cries of the barbarians, the whistle of another arrow barrage.

You close your eyes and floor the gas pedal with all your might....

Turn to page 70.

The man cries out as you haul him to the ground. You roughly spin him around and tear the hood away from his face.

He cries out in Arabic and raises his hands to plead with you to spare him. He holds up the small tray he is carrying, a tray of shoelaces he was taking to sell at the bazaar.

You realize at once that you've made a mistake. This man is no COBRA agent. You help him to his feet, but he screams. You realize too late that he is screaming to two nearby Cairo policemen. The shoelace salesman excitedly begins to tell them his story.

A few seconds later you are in police custody. As they drag you away you hear the gunshots again. You look down the street. It is only a pickup truck backfiring!

Your jail cell is small, damp, and dark. You pace back and forth nervously. "*Of course* my teammates will come to bail me out," you tell yourself. "They won't just leave me here to rot. I haven't been *that* nasty to them...."

Or have you?

THE END

Tutanh Harmak takes one more step across the dusty pyramid floor, falters, looks from side to side as if confused, and then falls face forward to the ground. You run to the mummy and impulsively grab its arm. It is completely lifeless once again.

Flint runs over to Dr. Wilmott. "Are you okay, Doctor?" he asks.

Wilmott looks strangely disappointed. He bends over the mummy and examines it carefully. "Tutanh Harmak has guarded his ancient secret for thousands of years," Wilmott says quietly. "I guess he wasn't about to reveal it to Serpentor now. He'd rather kill Serpentor than give up his secret." Wilmott shakes his head sadly.

Why is he so disappointed?

You don't care. Wearily, you rejoin your teammates. Your mission is accomplished. You're going home—with some whopping exploits to brag about nonstop when you get there!

Will anyone back at the Pit believe your stories? They'd better. And if they don't—well, they don't call you Bombshell for nothing, after all!

THE END

"Sci-Fi—let 'em have it!" you yell.

"No. It's at too close range," he tells you. "And there are too many of them. Lasers have to be aimed slowly and precisely."

You don't like to give up, but you have no choice. You stare out from the tank at the triumphant COBRAS. "Hey—who's the clown in the green snake hat?" you ask.

"It's Serpentor!" Mainframe tells you, sounding surprised. He punches a few keys on his computer. Information about Serpentor appears on the screen. "The word from our intelligence agents is that he is a COBRA creation. He was created with genetic materials from the bodies of the ten greatest warriors of all time!"

"Right, Mainframe. And do you believe in the Easter bunny, too?" you say sarcastically.

Mainframe ignores your sarcasm. "See that bald guy with the big mustache? That's the COBRA scientist who supposedly created him —Dr. Mindbender!"

"Ha ha! Who's his barber?" you scoff. "Hey, look—that Serpentor character doesn't look too happy."

Serpentor certainly *doesn't* appear happy. His eyes blazing behind the viper-toothed mask, he runs over to Dr. Mindbender and jerks him roughly from his vehicle....

Turn to page 46.

You run through the long corridor of the fortress, your rifles blazing.

"*Aaaaiiii!*" The last of the COBRA guards drops. You race past him into a large, brightly lit room.

A figure, hooded in blue, leaps up from a low table and runs to a hidden doorway in the far wall. "It's COBRA Commander!" Flint yells. "After him!"

"No wonder this place was guarded better than the secret formula for Coke!" you cry.

COBRA Commander makes his getaway, but the hidden fortress is now yours. "Not a bad day's work," you announce, sitting down at COBRA Commander's desk.

"I agree," says a deep voice. You look up to see a huge man wearing a flowing yellow cape. His face is hooded by a serpentine mask. It's the COBRA super-warrior, Serpentor!

Turn to page 81.

You aim your machine pistol at Mindbender and pull the trigger. Nothing happens! Angrily you toss the gun to the floor.

Mindbender gets over his surprise quickly. He lunges at you, arms outstretched, and pulls you down. The other members of the G.I. Joe Team rush into the room, but they're driven back by a barrage of COBRA weaponfire.

Mindbender is stronger than you thought. He drives a solid blow into your belly. Another, then another. Gunfire blazes all around you. The COBRAS seem to be gaining the upper hand.

Mindbender continues to pound you. You struggle to get away from him, but you can't.

You feel yourself growing weak....

Go on to page 61.

You use your final surge of energy to roll out from under Mindbender, pull him up, and drive a fist into his jaw. It isn't much of a punch, but it's enough to send him sprawling backward into a jagged edge of broken brick wall.

Mindbender utters a low moan and slumps unconscious to the ground.

You grab hold of the wall to support yourself. You've taken a bad pummeling. You look around and see that your teammates are still battling the Crimson Guards.

Dr. Wilmott stands in the corner, looking very confused and worried. You muster all of your strength and rush over to him.

"Don't worry, Doc," you say, grabbing his arm. "I'll get you outta here."

To your surprise, Wilmott pulls out of your grip and draws a pistol on you. *Fool!* he cries angrily.

Turn to page 48.

"Well…maybe we'd better make sure that nothing important is hidden here," Flint says. "Okay, Bombshell, it's fun time. Go ahead and wreck the joint!"

Gung-Ho, Roadblock, and Leatherneck gleefully join you as you begin blasting down the walls with your machine guns. They don't crumble easily. The building was constructed as a fortress.

"Hey—a tunnel!" you cry as a fallen wall reveals a narrow entranceway. "I knew we'd find something good! Let's go!"

You plunge into the dark tunnel. Its downward winding path leads into a low, empty cavern. The cavern leads into another tunnel which takes you deeper, deeper into the wet ground.

"Why did the COBRAS build this?" Flint wonders. "Or have these tunnels been here for ages?"

Turn to page 9.

Crack-crack.

"Let's go check out those shots," you say.

The four of you leap out of the jeep, leaving it in the middle of the narrow street, and run toward the sound. A man in a bright white business suit struggles to get out of your way and falls against a low wall. Two horses rear up, braying their surprise.

"This way!" you yell, turning back to direct your buddies. You hear a loud scream—

—as you run right into a vegetable cart and tumble headfirst into a pile of lettuce!

The furious cart owner continues to scream as his vegetables roll down the narrow street. You struggle to get up, but he angrily shoves you down again.

A crowd is beginning to form. You see two women with black veils over their faces—just like in the movies! You stand up and wipe hunks of crushed tomatoes off your uniform. Where are your teammates?

Turn to page 82.

"Hit the water!" you yell.

Just as the four of you leap into the tumbling brown water, you hear the roar of an engine. Arrows splash all around you as you plunge underwater, swimming hard away from the shore.

When you surface, you see a familiar sight —it's a G.I. Joe WHALE. The big hovercraft, its powerful guns blasting toward shore, roars up to you. The backup team has arrived just in time!

You and your teammates climb onto the WHALE. You look to the shore to see the barbarian army fleeing from the hovercraft's guns. "Hey, Bombshell—I always said you were all wet!" Flint says, dryly shaking his head.

You growl at him. "Thanks for the warm greeting, Flint. I'd toss you in, but they got laws about polluting the water here!"

"I ain't been shot at with bows and arrows since I was a kid," Roadblock says. "My brother and me—"

"Uh-oh!" you cry. "We don't have time to reminisce about the old days. We've got company!"

Skimming over the river is a heavily armed fleet of COBRA Water Moccasins, their surface torpedoes in place, ready to blow you from the water!

Turn to page 80.

You look over Flint's shoulder as he reads the printout of the message Mainframe intercepted. It reads:

DR. AND OLD EGYPTIAN ARE IN GOOD HANDS. ARE TRAVELING TO SWISS ALPS RETREAT AS PLANNED.

Some numbers follow, which appear to be latitude and longitude. The message is signed "CC."

COBRA Command?

"What do you make of this, Flint?" Mainframe asks.

"Can I finish my joke now?" you ask impatiently.

"If this is a message from COBRA Command, its meaning is real clear," Flint says, frowning. "We're heading to Cairo—and Dr. Wilmott and the mummy are on their way to the Alps!"

Turn to page 78.

You move in to finish him off, and he slams both fists into your forehead.

You crumble to the floor. You can't believe it—you're actually seeing stars!

Guns are blazing all over the room. Your eyes are swimming in flashing, flaring reds and yellows.

When you can finally focus, you see that Serpentor has run over to Mindbender's electronic machine. "*Stop!*" you yell. The effort makes your head throb.

You struggle to stand, but you are too dizzy. You squint your eyes and see Serpentor throw the switch!

"*No!*" you shout. The machine whirrs into action. You see a ribbon of electricity shoot out of the back. The whirr becomes a deafening squeal. The electrical current shoots to the very top of the pyramid—

And Tutanh Harmak takes its first stiff steps forward....

Turn to page 35.

You shove Sci-Fi out of the way and grab for the laser cannon release button. "No—wait! You don't understand!" Sci-Fi protests, trying to pull you away.

"I don't understand the meaning of the word *surrender*!" you tell him. You press the button.

But the laser cannon is perched too high for such a close-range target. A beam of red laser light shoots uselessly toward the sky.

The COBRA Ferrets respond with missile fire. Your adventure ends unhappily in a blaze of heat and white light.

It was a nice try, Bombshell. But even the best soldier sometimes needs to know the meaning of the word *surrender*! For now, you've learned the meaning of the word—

END

The barbarians shove you inside the narrow entrance to the COBRA headquarters. There Crimson Guards armed with machine pistols take over. You are led down a long dark corridor. It is hot and damp. The air smells stale and sour.

A masked figure steps out of a doorway and holds up a gloved hand. You recognize him immediately. It is Destro, a weapons dealer and COBRA ally. "Well, well..." He rubs his gloved hands together. "New recruits. Serpentor will be pleased. You have done well, Zartan!"

Zartan grins and shakes his head. "Serpentor doesn't need any more recruits," he tells Destro. "I think we should kill them before they cause any trouble."

Turn to page 12.

"We broke through!" Gung-Ho yells. "Keep going, Bombshell!"

"No. I thought I'd stop and have my oil checked!" you reply sarcastically. "Gee, where would I be without your advice, pal?"

The barbarians let out a high-pitched wail that sounds like an ambulance siren. It echoes eerily off the flat desert lands as they turn their horses and come after you.

The jeep engine chokes and sputters. It's probably getting clogged with sand. "Come on, come *on*!" you yell, jamming your foot on the gas and hoping you don't flood the engine.

Your teammates turn and fire their assault rifles at the onrushing barbarians. As the jeep finally jerks forward, it kicks up so much sand that it's hard to see. But by the sound of their constant wailing, you can tell the barbarians are closing in on you.

"Where is the backup team?" you wonder. You don't have long to think about them. You slam on the brakes. The jeep slides across the sand.

"Looks like it's swim time!" you tell your buddies, staring straight ahead.

The brown waters of the Nile River have blocked your escape.

Go on to page 71.

"Maybe we can find a boat," Gung-Ho yells, jumping out of the jeep to get a better look at the wide river.

"Yeah. Maybe the *Queen Mary* is docked over there," you reply with a scowl.

Turn to page 85.

Your decaying foe staggers toward you. You prepare to pounce. You time your leap. Just as you are about to begin, the door bursts open.

The lab blazes with laser fire! Flint, Mainframe, and Sci-Fi run in, their laser pistols flaring. "Aww, who invited *you* to my party?" you cry. You'd never let on that you're actually glad to see them!

Serpentor and Mindbender flee through a hidden door in the wall. The Crimson Guards are quickly defeated.

Triumphantly you lift the mummy off the floor in both hands and hold it high over your head. "*No! Don't!*" Flint yells to you. But he's too late. You heave the mummy at Mindbender's brain scanner machine.

Baaaarrrroooom!

The machine explodes with a blast that knocks you to the floor. As the debris settles, you climb to your feet.

"Way to go, Bombshell," Sci-Fi says sadly, shaking his head. "You just blew up a priceless scientific artifact."

"Fortunes of war, old buddy," you say, "fortunes of war."

Go on to page 73.

A few minutes later Dr. Wilmott revives, still dazed from having his brain waves copied. "My mummy—" are his first words. He looks around. He sees the pieces of cloth and ancient clay. "Oh, no," he says sadly. "Oh, no."

"He misses his mummy!" you say.

"Shut up, Bombshell," Flint says angrily. "Or we'll transfer *your* brain to a chimpanzee!"

"That would lower the chimp's IQ about a hundred points!" Sci-Fi adds.

Everyone has a good laugh at your expense. You shrug your shoulders and laugh right along with them. What the heck—this mission is over!

THE END

Standing in the secret entranceway, eaves-dropping on these two scheming COBRAS, you hear their astounding plan, and you quickly come to understand why Tutanh Harmak was stolen from the museum.

It seems that Tutanh Harmak went to his death thousands of years ago with the knowledge of how to unleash the awesome power of the pyramid. The secret of the pyramid was known only by members of ancient Egyptian royalty. Tutanh Harmak took that secret to his grave.

Now Mindbender plans to use the same reanimating techniques that brought Serpentor to life on the mummy. "I will bring the mummy to life," he tells a grinning Serpentor. "And when I do, his secret will be yours—and the powers of the pyramid will become *your* powers!"

Mindbender pulls a cone-shaped metal hood over the mummy's head and steps up to a large electronic machine.

You've heard—and seen—enough. Without consulting your G.I. Joe teammates to come up with a plan, you burst into the room.

Now—whom do you attack?

Mindbender? Turn to page 60.
Serpentor? Turn to page 28.

75

"Hey, this place is pretty modern for people who walk around in their bathrobes and pajamas!" you say as your jeep carries you past the tall skyscrapers of the central district.

"Bombshell, we can do without your dumb comments," Leatherneck growls.

"Who's gonna stop me?" you growl back. But you decide to let it drop. The broad avenue gives way to narrow, crowded streets lined with low wooden shacks. You screech to a halt to let a flock of sheep cross the street.

Suddenly, over the bleating of the sheep and the voices of the people in the street, you hear a *crack-crack-crack* sound. "Gunshots!" yells Leatherneck, grabbing his M-1. "Comin' from behind us!"

"Hold on just a darned minute!" you cry. Up ahead you see a robed figure duck into a dark tavern doorway. You catch a glimpse of the man's face. It looks very familiar to you. "Zartan!" you yell.

Is it the COBRA master of disguise—or are your eyes playing tricks on you? Should you chase after the man you think is Zartan—or should you investigate the gunshots?

Zartan? Turn to page 4.
Gunshots? Turn to page 63.

You decide to attack Mindbender. As he turns from his machine you leap at him. You knock him to the floor, but he drags you down with him. You struggle to overpower him. He fights hard, for a scientist.

He lands a solid punch to your ribs, and you cry out. You look up to see Serpentor rush to the brain scanner machine. "Stop!" you shout.

But you are too late. Serpentor pulls the switch!

Turn to page 86.

Still frowning, Flint rereads the message. "Of course, it could also be a trick," he says. "It wouldn't be the first time COBRA sent out a phony message for us to intercept."

"Yeah," you quickly agree. "The whole thing smells phony to me!"

"*Something* smells in here, for sure," Sci-Fi mutters.

"What did you say?" you snarl.

"Cool it," Flint orders. "We have a fast decision to make here. Is COBRA trying to throw us off the track—or is the mummy really on its way to the Alps?"

Which direction will the Joe Team head in next?

....

Toward the Swiss Alps? Turn to page 7.
On to Cairo as planned? Turn to page 38.

Serpentor is infuriated by your insolence. "Take him to Mindbender's lab!" he commands. "I'm going to use his brain cells in my barbarian soldiers. He has just the spirit they need to be *truly* barbaric fighting men!"

You try to break free again, but the guards overpower you and drag you down the corridor. "Give it to 'em, Bombshell!" you hear Gung-Ho yell. Then you are dragged through a doorway into a large lab filled with electronic machines.

A small, thin man has been strapped under a metal hood that is attached to one of the machines. You recognize him immediately as Dr. Wilmott. The stolen mummy also has a metal hood placed over its head.

Dr. Mindbender, grinning broadly under his thick black mustache, steps forward to greet Serpentor. "Just in time, my friend," Mindbender says. "I am about to transfer Wilmott's mind into the mummy. In a few moments, your old fighting buddy, Tutanh Harmak, will live again!"

"This is madness! Madness!" Wilmott cries from under the metal hood. Serpentor steps forward and silences him with a hard slap to the face.

"You may proceed," Serpentor tells Mindbender.

Turn to page 6.

Flint swivels the WHALE rocket launcher and blasts away at the approaching COBRA crafts.

Sci-Fi fires the laser cannon. But the hovercraft is moving too quickly and bobbing too much for him to aim it precisely enough to score a hit.

"Nice shootin', ace!" you yell as your assault rifle finds a bull's-eye—and then another. A Water Moccasin bursts into flames, its occupants diving into the river.

Mainframe spins the wheel, and the WHALE swerves away from a barrage of torpedo fire. Your rockets find their targets. More COBRAS hit the water. The other COBRAS realize they are facing defeat. They turn and flee over the silent waters.

"*Yo, Joe!*" you yell. "How sweet it is!"

"Aren't you forgetting a little something?" Flint asks, wiping the sweat off his forehead with his green beret.

"What's that?" you ask testily.

"We're not finished. We're here on a mission. We've got a job to do," Flint says.

"Oh. That." You'd almost forgotten.

Turn to page 87.

Serpentor gives a signal and a squadron of Crimson Guards rushes into the room, rifles aimed at your heads. You have no choice but to throw down your weapons.

"Not a bad day's work at all," says Serpentor, grinning. "I want to thank you boys for doing my work! I sent that message hoping you would fly here and destroy COBRA Commander's power base. Now COBRA is all mine —and the G.I. Joe Team did it for me!" His laughter echoes off the fortress walls.

You've done a great job, Bombshell—for Serpentor! And what is your reward? Luckily you get to close the book before you find out!

THE END

"Hey, Leatherneck! Gung-Ho!" you call to them. But no one can hear you over the loud voices, honking horns, and animal cries in the street.

They must have run ahead, you decide. So you take off, the angry cart owner still screaming and gesturing.

Holding your rifle in front of you, you twist your way through the crowd. A school bus has become stuck in a rut up ahead of you. The kids stick their hands out of the windows and wave as you run by.

You stop short when you see a man in a blue robe moving in the shadows. Is that a COBRA insignia on his sleeve? You follow him as he turns a corner into an even darker, narrower street.

You run up behind him and leap onto his back.

Turn to page 56.

As you watch this bizarre scene, it all becomes clear to you. First Mindbender created Serpentor, using cells from history's greatest warriors. He used the same process to build an army of barbarians for Serpentor. Now he's going to bring back Serpentor's ancient Egyptian buddy—with a new brain, courtesy of Dr. Wilmott!

You've got to try to stop Mindbender! As always, you don't bother to come up with a plan. You use your awesome strength to break free of the guards. Then, screaming like a wild man, you run into the middle of the lab. Now what?

....

Attack Mindbender? Turn to page 77.
Attack Serpentor? Turn to page 34.
Try to free Dr. Wilmott? Turn to page 52.

Zartan laughs and signals for his soldiers to take you prisoner. He leads the way along a trail that follows the path of the Nile River. A short while later, you reach your destination—a low, flat-roofed, unpainted wood building.

"This must be the place where they stashed Wilmott and the mummy," Gung-Ho whispers to you.

"Well, it ain't no disco!" you snarl back.

Turn to page 69.

Arrows splash into the water just a few yards off-target. The barbarian army is seconds away from you.

"Well—what's it gonna be?" Leatherneck says, raising his M-1 and pointing it toward the approaching army. "Stand and fight—or try to escape on the river?"

There's no time to debate. You have only seconds to decide!

Stand and fight? Turn to page 8.
Try to escape on the river? Turn to page 30.

A rush of electricity crackles through the room as the machine whirrs into motion. "*Aaaaiiiii!*" Dr. Wilmott screams in agony. His head slumps forward.

You and Mindbender stop your fight. You both stare wide-eyed as the ancient mummy lurches forward. Walking slowly at first, it picks up speed as it comes toward you with out-stretched arms.

Serpentor laughs gleefully. "Finish him, old friend!" he tells the mummy. "Defeat the soldier you see before you!"

The mummy comes at you. It looks rotten and decayed. You jump to your feet and prepare to fight it.

You may not win—but it'll know it's been in a fight!

Turn to page 72.

Using his computerized tracking unit, Mainframe locates the place where Dr. Wilmott and the mummy had been traced. It is a long, low building on a small sand hill near the river.

You ready your weapons and step onto land. "Hey—where is everybody?" Leatherneck asks. "No guards? No nothin'?"

You kick down the door and burst into the building, expecting to be greeted by COBRA weaponfire. Silence.

You search the entire building. There are signs that a lot of people were there recently. But the building is deserted now.

"Serpentor may dress like a snake," Flint says, "but he thinks like a *fox*. He suckered us."

"Whaddaya mean?" you bark.

"He kept us busy on the river while he and his soldiers escaped—along with Dr. Wilmott and the mummy. We thought we were out on the water winning a big victory. But all we were doing was blowing our mission."

You stare at each other in the deserted, silent building. You are tired and you are disappointed. And you all know the worst part is still to come. Facing Serpentor would have been a *breeze* compared to facing Hawk and telling him how you've failed!

THE END

You quickly revive Dr. Wilmott and tell him that the mummy turned on Serpentor. Wilmott isn't surprised. "Mindbender made one small mistake," he tells you. "When he gave the mummy my mind, he also gave it my feelings, my *loyalties*. He automatically filled Tutanh Harmak with deep feelings of hatred for Serpentor!"

The mummy lies lifeless on the lab floor. Wilmott bends over it, examining it carefully for damage. "Is it still alive, Doc?" Roadblock asks.

"No," Wilmott says thoughtfully. "Mindbender made a second mistake. Bringing an actual physical being back to life is a lot different from creating new beings from genetic materials. Mindbender is a genius, an evil genius. But even he couldn't keep this old fellow alive for long."

"Let's get outta here," you say. "This all reminds me of a horror movie."

"You *always* remind me of a horror movie, Bombshell!" Leatherneck scowls. "*It Came from Beneath a Rock!*"

"Gimme a break," you tell your laughing buddies. "Y'know, I didn't need you guys. I had it all under control in here!"

It isn't true, of course. But why let 'em think you're going soft?

THE END